The Littlest Easter Bunny

Written by
Brandi Dougherty

Illustrated by
Jamie Pogue

Cartwheel Books
An Imprint of Scholastic Inc.
New York

For my sister, Monica, even though
you're the biggest. — B.D.

To my mom and dad, for always helping me
pursue my dreams. Thank you. — J.P.

All rights reserved. Published by Scholastic Inc., *Publishers since 1920.* SCHOLASTIC, CARTWHEEL BOOKS, and associated logos are trademarks and/or registered trademarks of Scholastic Inc.

ISBN 978-1-338-32912-4

10 9 8 7 6 5 4 3 2 1   20 21 22 23 24

Printed in the U.S.A.   40
First printing, January 2020

Designed by Jess Tice-Gilbert

Penny was a bunny.
She lived with her family in a warren in Easter Town.
There were many bunnies in Penny's community,

but she was the littlest one.

It was springtime and Penny was excited.
This year she would get to help the town prepare for Easter!

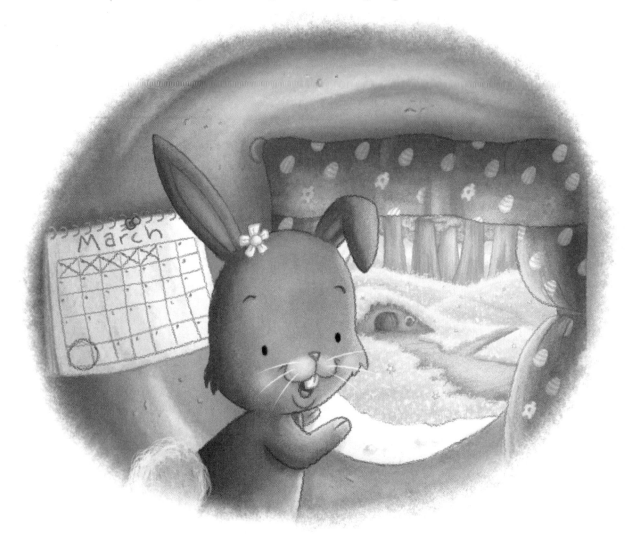

There were so many important jobs to do to get
the Easter Bunny ready for the holiday.

Penny just had to find the right one.

Penny's first stop was the egg-painting studio. These animals were artists! They painted all the eggs the Easter Bunny hid.

Penny's sister, Bea, showed her how to dip an egg in the dye.

But the vats of dye were very big ... "Oh, Penny!"

Penny's next stop was her brother's sweets shop.
Baxter made the biggest, most delicious marshmallow chicks
and chocolate bunnies in the whole town.

Baxter showed Penny how to pour the melty chocolate into the molds.

"Penny?" Baxter asked, looking around.

"Maybe you'll be better helping Momsy," Baxter suggested.

Penny hopped to her mother's basket-weaving workshop.
The Easter Bunny needs a lot of baskets for his deliveries!

Weaving was more complicated than it looked.
Penny got dizzy and spun in a circle. Then, crash!

"Oh dear," said Penny's mother.
"Why don't you go see Popsy?"

Penny's father supervised the crew who filled the Easter baskets with treats.

"Add the grass, then the chocolate bunnies, then the eggs with special surprises inside," Popsy instructed.

The other animals worked so fast!
Penny's tiny paws couldn't keep up.

Popsy peered into Penny's
almost-empty basket.
"Maybe next year, sweet girl,"
he said gently.

Penny hopped outside. But it wasn't a happy, snappy springtime hop. It was a sad, pouty cloudy-day hop. There had to be one special Easter job she could do, even if she was little.

Just then, Penny heard a noise coming from an azalea bush.
She peeked inside to find Peck the chick.

And he was little, just like Penny!

Peck was pouty-sad, too.
"All the other chicks have found their special Easter jobs," he explained.
"Except for me."

Penny didn't like to see someone sad. She thought about how to make
Peck happy. Then she got an idea big enough for both of them!

With a little help from Penny's family, Penny and Peck started making their own Easter baskets filled with treats.

And the baskets were little — just like them!

Easter day was almost here.
The whole town was bustling about helping prepare
the Easter Bunny for the big morning.

Suddenly, Bea and Baxter hopped past. "The Easter Bunny's
egg hiders caught spring fever! They can't go with him!"

Penny and Peck looked at each other. "We can do it!" Penny cried.
"You're too little," Baxter said.
"The Easter Bunny needs little helpers," Penny argued.
"We can find the best hiding spots."

Penny and Peck sprang into action.
They took their mini baskets to the Easter Bunny's office.
They told him all the reasons why they were the perfect egg hiders and showed him the tiny treasures they'd made for kids who are little, just like them.

The Easter Bunny listened quietly. Finally, he cleared his throat and said, "I think you might be right!"

Penny and Peck had the best time ever helping the Easter Bunny hide all the eggs. They found new and clever hiding spots. And their mini Easter baskets were perfect for the littlest kids to find.

They returned to Easter Town with big smiles and even bigger stories to tell. Their families were so proud!

It turned out that Penny and Peck were not too little to have important job on Easter.
But more than that, they were not too little to make a friend — because sometimes the most special things are also the littlest.